"What're those clippers for?" asked Tooter. "I don't need a haircut."

"Maybe not," said Aunt Sally. "But your show animal does."

"Pepperoni? What are you talking about?"

"Before you show a goat at the county fair, you shave off all its hair."

Tooter backed off. "No way. I am *not* going to shave a goat."

"If you don't shave a goat, you can't show a goat. If you don't show a goat, you can't win a blue ribbon."

Blue Ribbon Blues

A Tooter Tale

by Jerry Spinelli

illustrated by Donna Nelson

A STEPPING STONE BOOK™

Random House 🏠 New York

To the grandkids, every one of you.

Kathy Morgan—and her beloved goats—were
a big help in writing this story.   *—J.S.*

Text copyright © 1998 by Jerry Spinelli.
Illustrations copyright © 1998 by Donna Nelson.
All rights reserved under International and Pan-American Copyright
Conventions. Published in the United States by Random House, Inc.,
New York, and simultaneously in Canada by Random House of Canada
Limited, Toronto.

http://www.randomhouse.com/

Library of Congress Cataloging-in-Publication Data
Spinelli, Jerry.
Blue ribbon blues / by Jerry Spinelli.
p. cm. "A Stepping Stone book." SUMMARY: When Tooter Pepperday
and her family move to her aunt's farm, she decides to show everyone
and win a blue ribbon at the county fair.
ISBN 0-679-88753-9 (pbk.) — ISBN 0-679-98753-3 (lib. bdg.)
[1. Farm life—Fiction. 2. Fairs—Fiction. 3. Family life—Fiction.
4. Aunts—Fiction.] I. Nelson, Donna Kae, ill. II. Title. PZ7.S75663Bl
1998 [Fic]—dc21 97-5659

Printed in the United States of America 10 9 8 7 6 5 4 3 2 1
A STEPPING STONE BOOK is a trademark of Random House, Inc.

Contents

1

911

The policeman got into his car and drove off. Mrs. Pepperday waved from the porch. "Thank you, Officer! Have a nice day."

When the police car was out of sight, Mrs. Pepperday stopped smiling. She went into the house and stood at the foot of the stairway. "Tooter!" she called. She waited a moment. In her hand was a paintbrush, tipped with blue paint. She waved the brush in the air. "Tooter!" she shouted again, louder this time.

Chuckie came running. "Is Tooter in trouble again, Mom?"

"One guess," said Mrs. Pepperday.

Mrs. Pepperday stormed up the stairs. Chuckie followed close behind. They found Mr. Pepperday in his office. He was sitting at his computer, writing.

"Have you seen Tooter?" asked Mrs. Pepperday.

Mr. Pepperday turned around. "No. What's she done now?"

"She called 911, that's what. A policeman was here."

Just then a voice came from above. "You dumb chicken!"

"She's in the attic!" Chuckie cried.

Mrs. Pepperday and Chuckie climbed the stairs to the attic. They were joined by Harvey, their rusty, shaggy dog.

In the attic they found Tooter and Eggbert. Eggbert was two months old. Eggbert had been hatched from an egg. Eggbert was a chicken.

Tooter made a stern face. She pointed at Eggbert and said, "Sit!"

Eggbert ran off to the corner. Harvey sat.

Tooter growled at Harvey. "Not you, dog." She threw up her hands. "See, Mom? This dumb chicken won't do anything I say."

Mrs. Pepperday made a stern face of her own. "Is that why you called 911?"

"Of course," said Tooter, surprised that her mother would ask.

"911 is for emergencies."

Tooter sighed. "Mom, you think I don't know that? Look—" She pointed to Eggbert, who was toddling across the bare wood floor. "That chicken is two months old and *still* won't obey its mother. He hid under the old bed and wouldn't come out. If that's not an emergency, what is?"

Mrs. Pepperday held up a finger. "One, you are *not* that chicken's mother. You were simply there when it was hatched." She held up another finger. "Two, a chicken is not a dog. You can't teach it tricks. And three, hiding under a bed is *not* a police emergency."

She poked a finger in Tooter's face. "*Don't* do it again."

Chuckie pointed and grinned. "Yeah, *don't* do it again."

Tooter grabbed Chuckie's finger. She put it in her mouth. Mrs. Pepperday warned, "Tooter, don't you dare bite."

Tooter rolled her eyes.

Harvey arfed.

At last Tooter released the finger. "I wasn't going to bite it anyway," she said. Chuckie and Harvey ran down the stairs.

Mrs. Pepperday went down a step, then turned back to Tooter. "Would you like some advice from your mother?"

Tooter nodded.

"Don't holler at Eggbert. And especially don't call him names. Mothers don't do things like that."

"But you said I'm not his mother."

Mrs. Pepperday smiled. "I didn't say you couldn't pretend."

2

Mama Tooter

Tooter sat down on her father's desk.

"What are you writing today, Dad?" she asked.

Mr. Pepperday wrote books for children.

"A new story," he said. He rested his fingers on the keyboard. "Just started it."

"What's it about?"

"Oh," he said, "it's about a girl."

"What's her name?"

"Haven't decided yet."

"What's the story about?"

Mr. Pepperday folded his hands over his

stomach. "Well, I haven't figured it all out yet. I think I'll start with the girl moving from her home in the suburbs to a farm in the country."

Tooter's eyes opened wide. "Dad, that's me!"

Mr. Pepperday laughed. "Not really. Remember, it's just a story. It's made up. It's not real life."

Tooter's smile drooped. "I wish you could make up my real life for me."

Mr. Pepperday squeezed her knee. "What's the matter, Toot?"

Tooter slumped. "Eggbert doesn't like me."

"How do you know what Eggbert is feeling?"

"I can tell," said Tooter. "If he liked me, he would listen to me."

"Doesn't listen, huh?"

"Nope. No matter what I tell him to do, he doesn't do it. He never obeys me." She threw up her arms. "His *own* mother!"

Mr. Pepperday took Tooter's hands in his. He patted them. "Tooter, I'm afraid I have some shocking news for you. Eggbert is a chicken. He is not your son. You are not his mother."

"Dad, I *know* that!" Tooter scolded him. "But Mom said I can pretend."

"Oh, well, then," said Mr. Pepperday. "By all means, pretend away."

"Can you help me, Dad?" Tooter asked.

Mr. Pepperday folded his arms, bowed his head, and closed his eyes.

"Dad," said Tooter. "You can't go to sleep now!"

"I'm not," said Mr. Pepperday. "I'm thinking. Shhh."

Tooter remained silent while her father

thought. At last he opened his eyes. "Your mother used to sing to you."

Tooter brightened. "A lullaby?"

"No. Not a lullaby. But it's a song everybody knows."

"What?" said Tooter.

"'The Star-Spangled Banner.'"

Tooter laughed. "You're kidding." She looked at her father's face. "Right?"

Mr. Pepperday shook his head. "Nope. Not kidding. You hated lullabies. 'The Star-Spangled Banner' was the only song that put you to sleep. When you started to talk, you called it 'The Tar-Bangled Banner.'"

Tooter shrugged. "Okay, I guess it's worth a try." She went back up the stairs.

Mr. Pepperday heard Tooter singing in the attic.

"Oh! say, can you see…"

Mr. Pepperday smiled at the sound of his

daughter's voice singing the national anthem.

"...and the home of the brave?"

What followed was definitely not singing.

"Sleep, chicken!"

Then came footsteps stomping down the stairs and into his office.

"Dad—"

Mr. Pepperday cut her off. "Okay," he said, "how about this? Eggbert is a chicken, right?"

"Right."

"So maybe Eggbert will only listen to another chicken."

"Great thinking, Dad," said Tooter. "Except for one little thing. I'm not a chicken."

Mr. Pepperday nodded. "Not a real chicken. But remember, you're not a real mother, either. Just a pretend mother. So maybe what we need here is..." He paused.

"A pretend chicken!" Tooter chimed in.

Mr. Pepperday had a sly grin on his face. "And isn't there an old feather pillow someplace in the attic?"

Tooter's eyes widened. She shot up the stairs.

Later that afternoon Mr. Pepperday rounded up the family. He fetched Aunt Sally from the honey house. He called in Chuckie and Harvey from the barnyard. He made Mrs. Pepperday stop painting the porch.

He told them all to be very quiet. He led them up the stairs to the attic. Slowly he opened the door.

"Ba-*bawlk!* Ba-*bawlk!*"

It was Tooter. Squawking like a chicken. Flapping like a chicken. Looking like a chicken in the pillow feathers she had glued to a pillowcase sack dress. While Tooter trotted in circles, Eggbert pecked at the floor.

Mr. Pepperday closed the door. Everyone held in their laughter until they were downstairs.

When Aunt Sally finished laughing, she said, "I think I know what that girl needs. And it's *not* a chicken."

3

Part One

Tooter climbed into Aunt Sally's pickup. "Where are we going?" she said.

Aunt Sally started the engine. The pickup rolled forward. "To find you a friend." She turned onto Frog Hollow Road.

"You think that's what I need?"

"I do."

"I'll tell you what I need," said Tooter. "I need a pizza. I haven't tasted pizza since we moved here. That's two whole months!"

Aunt Sally goggled at Tooter. "Horrors!" She waved at a passing pickup. "You know what you'll really need if you're going to live on my farm?"

"What's that?"

"You'll need to become a real farmer."

"I know. I want to," said Tooter. "But not if it means wearing a hat like that."

Aunt Sally acted surprised. "You don't like my hat?" She took off her straw hat and plunked it onto Tooter's head.

Tooter made a face. "Ugh!" She plunked the hat back onto her aunt's head.

"Okay," said Aunt Sally. "No hat. But I do have a plan for making a farmer out of you. It has three parts."

"What are they?" said Tooter.

"You'll find out," said Aunt Sally. She turned off the road into a dusty driveway. "Part one...coming up."

Aunt Sally parked the pickup in front of a large white house. They got out. Aunt Sally cupped her hands and called, "Helloooo there!"

A lady leaned out of an upstairs window. "Hello, yourself. Is this Tooter?"

"Fresh from the city."

"Hi, Tooter," said the lady. She waved her arm. "Jack is out there somewhere. Probably with Cleo."

Aunt Sally waved and walked off. Tooter followed.

"Who's Jack?" said Tooter.

"Your neighbor. Jack Hafer. He's your age. He can be your friend. That's part one—get you a friend. I called Mrs. Hafer and told her we were coming over."

"What if he doesn't like me?"

"He will. And he'll be good for you. He's lived on this farm all his life. He can teach you a lot."

As they walked around the barn, Aunt

Sally said, "Well, chuck my chickens. Look at that."

Before them stood a boy and an animal. All they could see of the animal was its hind end.

The boy looked up. "Miss Sally," he called, "can you help me?"

Aunt Sally and Tooter trotted over. Now the problem was clear. The animal was a goat, one of the few farm creatures that Tooter recognized. Its head was stuck between two rails of a wooden fence.

"I can't get it out," said the boy.

Tooter had an idea. "Pull the tail," she said.

The boy gave Tooter a dirty look.

As the goat struggled, its front hooves knocked noisily against the fence.

"You hold the neck still," Aunt Sally told the boy. "I'll work the head."

They twisted and tugged. The goat bawled and stomped. At last its head was free.

The boy gave the goat a smack on the rump. "Bad, Cleo. She's always doing that."

The goat walked off to graze.

The boy turned to Tooter. "You *don't* pull a goat's tail," he said sharply.

"See?" Tooter said to Aunt Sally. "He doesn't like me already. Part one is *not* going to work." She walked off.

Aunt Sally caught her by her back pocket. "Hold on there, missy." She pulled Tooter back and turned her around. "You two haven't even been introduced yet. Jack, this is Tooter. She's your new neighbor."

"Tooter?" said Jack. "What kind of name is that?"

"See?" said Tooter. She tried to walk off, but Aunt Sally still had her by the back pocket.

"Tooter is a nickname," Aunt Sally told Jack. "And a fine nickname it is. Tooter's family lives with me now. They moved here from the city. Tooter wants to become a good farmer." She tapped the bill of Jack's cap. "And I figure you're just the one to teach her."

Jack groaned. "Miss Sally, I already have

lots of chores to do. Plus I have to get Cleo ready for the fair."

Tooter perked up. "What fair?"

"The county fair," said Jack. "I'm entering Cleo in the goat competition." He lifted his chin. "I always win."

"Well," said Tooter, "poo-poo-pee-doo for you."

Jack just stared at her.

"Maybe I'll enter too," said Tooter, lifting her own chin. "Maybe my chicken will beat your goat."

"Hah!" said Jack. "Maybe *not*. Chickens and goats don't compete together."

"Yeah, well, you're lucky they don't," said Tooter. "Because if they did, my chicken would beat the pants off your goat."

"Yeah?" said Jack.

"Yeah," said Tooter.

"What can your chicken do?"

"Whatever I tell it," said Tooter. "It sleeps. It sits."

Jack scoffed. "Yeah, right."

"And it sings 'The Star-Spangled Banner.'"

Jack laughed. "And my *goat* sings 'Take Me Out to the Ball Game.'"

"Yeah? Well, my *chicken* plays Ping-Pong with me."

"Yeah? Well, my *goat* plays Frisbee with *me*."

"My *chicken* tap-dances."

"My *goat* runs the vacuum cleaner."

"My...my..." Tooter couldn't help herself. She burst out laughing.

So did Jack.

So did Aunt Sally. "Okay, you goofballs," she said. "I guess you're introduced. Say good-bye to each other."

"Good-bye, goat boy," said Tooter.

Jack grinned. "Good-bye, chicken girl!"

4

No Sprout

"So, that was part one," said Tooter. They were back out on Fox Hollow Road. "What's part two?"

"Alfalfa Sprouts," said Aunt Sally.

"Alfalfa Sprouts? What's that?"

"You'll see tonight," said Aunt Sally.

They rode in silence for a minute. Then Tooter said, "Aunt Sally, do you think I could win a blue ribbon? Like Part One Jack?"

Aunt Sally laughed. "Sure. If you work hard."

"But how could I ever win anything with Eggbert?"

"Who says it has to be a chicken?" said Aunt Sally. "We have a perfectly fine goat in the pasture."

"But that's what Part One Jack has," said Tooter. "And he always wins. My goat could *never* beat his goat."

Aunt Sally took her eyes from the road long enough to stare at Tooter. "Well, bless my bunions. I never would have thunk it. I do believe young Miss Pepperday is afraid of losing."

Tooter looked out the window at the passing fields and silos. "Young Miss Pepperday isn't afraid of anything," she muttered.

That evening after dinner Aunt Sally and Tooter were back in the pickup.

"Okay," said Tooter. "I'm tired of waiting. Now what are the Alfalfa Sprouts?"

"The Alfalfa Sprouts are a group of farmers' kids," said Aunt Sally. "They're all under twelve years old. They meet at the Grange. They raise their own animals and crops to show at the county fair."

"Will Part One Jack be there?"

"I reckon. Jack's been a Sprout for years. But plenty of others will be there too."

"Girls?"

"Lots."

The pickup stopped at the Grange. Aunt Sally took Tooter inside and left her with the leader, a lady with a "Miss Piggy for President" button.

When Aunt Sally left, Tooter was smiling.

When Aunt Sally came back an hour later, Tooter was frowning.

Tooter climbed into the pickup. "What's that smell?"

Aunt Sally sniffed. "I don't smell anything. So, how'd it go?"

"Not so good," Tooter replied.

"How so?"

"Because I had to stand up in front of everybody and say, 'Hi. My name is Tooter Pepperday. I'm a Sprout!' And everybody waved back and shouted, 'Howdy, Sprout!'"

"So?" said Aunt Sally. "They were just being friendly."

"That's not the point," said Tooter. She sniffed and looked behind her seat. "I don't like being called a Sprout. It sounds like I'll grow up to be a turnip."

Aunt Sally sighed. "Well, if that's how you feel, I guess you don't have what it takes to be a farmer. I guess that's all you want to be...a turnip." She tweaked Tooter's nose. "Turnip Tooter."

Tooter laughed. "Hey," she said, "I forgot. What's part three?"

Aunt Sally turned into the driveway. She

shrugged. "What does a turnip care about part three?"

"Tell me!" Tooter pleaded.

Aunt Sally turned off the motor and got out. Leaning into the open window, she said, "While you were Sprouting, I drove twenty miles." She was grinning now. "Part three is under your seat. That's what you've been smelling."

Tooter reached down and pulled out a box. Square. Flat. Warm. A smell she hadn't smelled in two months. Her joyful scream reached every corner of the farm.

"*Pizzaaaaaaaaa!*"

5

A Very Fine Goat

Tooter was having breakfast with Aunt Sally the next morning when they heard a loud commotion. A terrible squawking.

"The chickens!" said Aunt Sally.

They ran outside.

Three chickens fussed on the roof of the coop. The others were in the branches of a nearby tree. Tooter saw something move at the top of the hill. A flash of hind legs and tail disappeared into the woods.

"Harvey!" she called.

"Arf!" Harvey replied.

Tooter turned. Harvey was right behind her.

So if Harvey was here, then what was up *there?*

Aunt Sally was staring at several brown feathers on the ground. She looked toward the hill. "Coyote," she said.

"Coyote?" said Tooter. "You mean like Wile E. Coyote and the Roadrunner?"

Aunt Sally picked up a feather. "Yep. Only this coyote is real. And he *ain't* funny."

"I thought coyotes were out west," said Tooter.

"They're showing up in these parts," said Aunt Sally. "Jack Hafer's father said he saw one the other day."

Tooter stared at the feather in her aunt's hand. Suddenly she realized what had happened. "The coyote took a chicken!"

"Bingo."

Tooter clung to her aunt. She looked fearfully at the hilltop. "Do they take kids too?"

"No," said Aunt Sally. "But they scare the devil out of goats."

They found Aunt Sally's goat standing on its hind legs under a tree. Its front hooves pawed at the trunk, ripping bark.

Tooter forgot her own fear. She helped Aunt Sally bring the goat's front feet down. The poor thing's eyes were bulging with terror. It was trembling in her hands. She petted it. She talked to it. "It's okay...it's okay. The coyote is gone. You're safe."

She led the goat back to the barnyard. She discovered she didn't want to leave it.

"Aunt Sally," she said, "what's the goat's name?"

Aunt Sally scratched her ear. "Guess it don't rightly have a name. I usually just call it 'hey you.'"

Tooter stepped back to look the goat over. It was the color of dirty white socks before they went into the washer. She was thinking of naming it "Socks" when suddenly she burped. And the burp tasted like last night's pizza.

"I got it!" she cried. She leaned in nose to nose with the goat. "Pepperoni!"

Aunt Sally nodded. "Pepperoni Pepperday. I like it."

Now that Tooter had named the goat, she felt closer to it. She put her arm around its neck. "This is a nice goat," she said.

"A fine goat," said Aunt Sally.

"A very fine goat," said Tooter.

"Too bad nobody else ever gets to see her," said Aunt Sally. "Stuck away in this here barnyard."

Tooter looked at Aunt Sally. Aunt Sally was grinning. Tooter said, "I know what you're thinking."

Aunt Sally looked surprised. "And just *what* am I thinking?"

Tooter pointed at her aunt.

"*You* think I want to show Pepperoni at the county fair."

"Well, bumble my bees," said Aunt Sally. "A mind reader. Anything else?"

Tooter put her hands on her hips. "And you're going to help me."

Aunt Sally saluted. "Yes, ma'am."

6

Learning to Walk

That afternoon they stood in front of Pepperoni.

"Now this," said Aunt Sally, "is a goat."

Tooter laughed. "I know."

"You also have to know the parts of your goat," said Aunt Sally. "You'll be tested at the show."

"No problem," said Tooter. "I already know the parts." She pointed. "Legs. Tail. Mouth. Nose. Ears. Udder."

Aunt Sally nodded. "Very good. Now where are the wattles?"

Tooter stared at Aunt Sally. "Wattles? What're wattles?"

"You tell me," said Aunt Sally.

Tooter looked over the goat. She whispered in its ear. "Pepperoni, where're your wattles?"

Pepperoni didn't answer.

Tooter stepped back. Frowning, she studied the animal. "Okay," she said. "I give up. Where're the wattles?"

Aunt Sally pointed to two furry flaps of skin, one on each of Pepperoni's cheeks. She grinned. "Wattles."

A bicycle came around the barn and clattered through the dust. It was Jack Hafer.

"What's he doing here?" said Tooter.

"He's the real goat expert," said Aunt Sally. "He won the blue ribbon last year. I asked him to come over and teach you how to show your goat."

When Jack came near, Tooter grabbed his

cheek and shook it. "Wattle!" she declared.

Jack did the same thing to Tooter. "Wattle yourself."

Aunt Sally laughed. "Well, it beats shaking hands."

"My goat has a name now," Tooter said. "It's Pepperoni."

"Pepperoni?" said Jack. "What kind of name is that?"

Tooter ignored the question. "And Pepperoni is going to be in the goat show. And she's going to win the blue ribbon."

Jack laughed. "*Your* goat is going to beat *my* goat? I don't think so."

"Not only that," said Aunt Sally, "but you are going to teach Tooter how to show her goat."

"But, Miss Sally," said Jack, "why should I help somebody else beat my own goat?"

"Because you want your new neighbor to be a fine farmer, just like yourself," said Aunt Sally.

Tooter batted her eyelashes. "And because I'm so nice."

Aunt Sally clapped her hands. "Okay, you two. Get down to work. I've got honey to pour." She handed the goat over to Jack and headed for the honey house.

"Guess what?" Tooter said to Jack. "A coyote ate one of our chickens."

Jack shook his head grimly. "Here too, huh? Last week it got one of my rabbits."

"Aunt Sally says they don't go after kids."

"I sure hope not," said Jack.

Tooter had had enough talk of coyotes. "So," she said, "are you going to teach me how to show my goat?"

Jack shrugged. "Why not? I can teach you all Miss Sally wants, but your goat will never beat my goat."

Tooter whispered in Pepperoni's ear. "Hear that, Pep? Are you gonna let him say that to you? Let's show him who's the best goat around here."

Jack just shook his head. "Can we begin now?"

Tooter stood at attention. She saluted. "Yes, *sir*."

Jack pulled Pepperoni along by the yellow plastic rope around her neck. "This is how you walk the goat." He led the goat in a circle. "Walk slow, like this."

"What if my goat wants to walk fast?" Tooter asked.

"Make her walk slow," said Jack. "Show her who's boss."

Tooter wagged a finger in Pepperoni's face. "Hear that, Pep? I'm the boss."

Jack went on. "Keep her head steady, close to you."

"Close to me?" said Tooter. "How close is close? What if she sneezes on me?"

Jack groaned. "She won't."

"But what if she *does?*" Tooter insisted. "Should I bring a hankie?"

Jack glared at her. "Yes, *yes*. Bring a

hankie. Bring *ten* hankies. Now can I con-
tinue?"

Tooter curtsied. "Be my guest."

"Okay," said Jack. "You're walking slow.
See? You're keeping her head close to you.
And steady. And don't pull her head down.

Keep it high."

"Why?" said Tooter.

"Because you're supposed to look proper," said Jack.

Tooter walked around with her nose in the air. "This isn't proper. This is snooty."

"Whatever," said Jack. "And don't look at the goat."

"Don't look?" Tooter screeched. "What kind of rule is that?"

Jack said, "How do I know? It's a rule, so just obey it."

"But what if Pepperoni looks at me?"

"She won't."

"But what if she *does?* Am I supposed to ignore my own goat? That's rude."

Jack faced the honey house. "Miss Sally!" he called. "Your niece is being silly! She won't listen!"

"He's being grouchy!" Tooter added.

Aunt Sally's voice came from the honey house. "Be nice!"

Tooter wagged her finger in Jack's face. "See? Be nice."

Jack bit his lip. He took a deep breath and went on with the lesson. He showed

Tooter how to stand the goat for the judge's inspection. "Front and back legs apart," he said. "Form a perfect rectangle."

"I like triangles," said Tooter.

"Fine," growled Jack. "Then get yourself a three-legged goat."

Tooter laughed. "Hey, that was a good one. You're a funny farmer, Jack."

"I'm a blue-ribbon farmer too," Jack shot back.

Tooter poked him in the arm. "We'll see about that."

7

Pepperoni Parts

After Jack left, Tooter found her father at his computer. "Working on your story about the girl who moves to a farm?" she said.

"Yep."

"Do you have it all figured out yet?"

"I can always use a good idea." He looked up at her. "Know anybody who has one?"

Tooter grinned. "Mmm, I might." She sat on his desk. "How about this? The girl has a goat. She names it Pepperoni."

"Why not Baloney or Salami?"

"Dad, be serious."

"Sorry."

"Okay. So, she meets this boy from the farm next door. And he's supposed to be a real hotshot. His goat wins the blue ribbon every year at the county fair. And he's grouchy to the girl, even though she's really, really nice to him. And so she decides to teach him a lesson. She enters *her* goat in the county fair. And"—Tooter clapped her hands —"she wins the blue ribbon!"

Mr. Pepperday nodded. "Sounds good," he said. "But I think one thing is missing."

"What's that?" said Tooter.

Mr. Pepperday scrolled down to a blank screen. He tapped on the keyboard. Two words appeared on the screen:

```
hard work
```

"Right, Dad," said Tooter. "I didn't forget. It

just slipped my mind. Here, I'll help you out."
She climbed onto his lap. Searching the keys
letter by letter, she tapped out a paragraph:

```
    The girl worked hard
every day with her goat.
She taught the goat to
stand like a perfect
rectangle. And she taught
it lots of other stuff. The
goat won the blue ribbon.
And the girl was famous.
```

She hopped off her father's lap. "Okay, Dad,
you can take it from there."

Tooter went outside. As she walked
through the barnyard, she couldn't tell which
chicken was Eggbert. They all looked alike.
And all of them ignored her.

But not Pepperoni. Seeing her coming, the

goat walked over to meet her. Tooter stroked her high, bony nose. She waggled her wattles. She looked into the goat's yellow, slotted eyes, so different from her own. Pepperoni ate some grass from her hand.

She whispered, "We're pals, aren't we, Pep?"

Pepperoni seemed to nod.

"And we're going to work hard and win that blue ribbon, aren't we?"

She put her ear to Pepperoni's mouth. She thought she heard the goat say *yes*.

Just then Chuckie and Harvey came running over. Chuckie was holding a book. He handed it to her. "Aunt Sally says you're supposed to study this. It's about goat parts."

Chuckie and Harvey ran off.

Tooter opened the book. On one page she found a drawing. It showed the parts of a goat.

"Okay, Pep," said Tooter. "These are your

pin bones." She pointed to spots on either side of Pepperoni's tail. She spoke clearly and slowly into Pepperoni's ear. She figured her goat should learn her own parts.

"And this is your dewclaw." She pointed to a spot just above Pepperoni's hoof. "That's a funny one," she said to herself. "Wonder if I have one of those." She pulled up her pants leg and pulled down her sock. "Nope," she said. "Just the old anklebone."

She pronounced and pointed out other parts.

"Stifle."

"Chine."

"Withers."

"Fetlock."

And, of course, "udder" and "wattles," which she already knew.

She walked around the goat pasture, studying the parts. A great way to test herself

came to mind. She ran into the house and returned with a pad of yellow Post-It notes. She wrote down each part name on a sheet. She pressed each part name where she thought it belonged on Pepperoni's body. When she checked the drawing in the book, she'd gotten them all right!

Behind her she heard laughter. And arfing.

Her mother stood there, paintbrush in hand, with Chuckie and Harvey. When her mother stopped laughing, she said, "I guess I owe Chuckie an apology. When he told me you wallpapered your goat, I didn't believe him. Now I do!"

8

Haircut

Every day Tooter and Pepperoni worked hard. They pretended the barnyard was a show ring. They practiced walking properly. Tooter taught Pepperoni how to stand perfectly still with her feet in a perfect rectangle. She trimmed Pepperoni's hooves and gave her a bath with a hose and scrub brush.

Two days before the county fair, Aunt Sally came to Tooter with hair clippers. "What're those for?" asked Tooter. "I don't need a haircut."

"Maybe not," said Aunt Sally. "But your show animal does."

"Pepperoni? What are you talking about?"

"Before you show a goat, you shave off all its hair. Didn't Jack tell you?"

"No, he didn't tell me."

"Well, I'm telling you now." She held out the clippers. "Here you go."

Tooter backed off. "No way. I am *not* going to shave a goat."

"If you don't shave a goat, you can't show a goat. If you don't show a goat, you can't win a blue ribbon."

Tooter said nothing. She allowed herself to be led to the pasture, where Pepperoni was munching grass. Aunt Sally flipped a switch. The clippers buzzed. "Just like shaving a head bald," she said. "Except you do it all over."

"*All* over?" said Tooter.

"All over. The whole shebang. Whiskers. Eyebrows. Inside the ears."

Tooter shrieked. "*Eyebrows!* Inside the

ears!" The thought of it made her own ears tickle.

"Come to think of it," said Aunt Sally, "there is one little spot you can let be."

"What's that?"

Aunt Sally went to Pepperoni's back end. "The tip of the tail. Leave about an inch there. So there's a nice little pom-pom on the end." She waved the clippers. "All right, pay attention. Here's how you do it."

Aunt Sally ran the clippers along Pepperoni's neck. Hair sprinkled to the ground. A strip of creamy white skin appeared. Aunt Sally handed the clippers to Tooter. "Your turn."

It took Tooter an hour just to shave the rest of Pepperoni's neck. She was afraid of hurting Pepperoni, but the goat stood still. She seemed to enjoy the haircut. Tooter was fascinated by the creamy smoothness of the

shaved skin. She rubbed it with her hand.
Then with her cheek. She hugged the goat.
She whispered, "You are the world's most
beautiful goat, Pepperoni Pepperday."

By afternoon the haircut was done. Tooter
left Pepperoni in the pasture. "Now don't you
get dirty," she said.

On the way back to the house, Tooter

heard squawking in the chicken coop. *Uh-oh,* she thought. *Coyote?* A chicken ran out of the coop, but no coyote followed. All was now silent inside the coop.

Tooter tiptoed to the doorway. She peeked inside. Her little brother was bending over a nest. A can of paint sat on the floor. A brush was in his hand.

"Chuckie?" she said. "What are you doing?"

Chuckie turned. He held up an egg. The egg was blue. He grinned. "Mom said I can use the rest of the paint. I'm painting eggs."

"So I see," said Tooter. It was kind of funny, so Tooter decided not to tattle on him.

Tooter dropped by her father's office. He was pecking away as usual. "I have a new idea for your story, Dad. The girl shaves her goat. Except for a pom-pom on its tail. The shaving takes hours and hours. You'll probably need a whole chapter for it."

Mr. Pepperday waved. "Thanks for the advice."

Tooter went to her room. She picked out the clothes she would wear for the county fair. She practiced her proper walk in front of the mirror.

Before dinner Mrs. Pepperday sent Tooter out to the garden for a cucumber. Every cucumber she reached for was blue. So were several tomatoes and a once-yellow squash.

On her way to report to her mother, Tooter noticed blue paint on the fence. And on the water bucket. And on the grass. And...

Tooter screamed.

A white animal with blue stripes was grazing in the pasture. It looked like a cartoon zebra.

"Pepperoni!"

9

No!

Tooter scrubbed Pepperoni's hide for an hour. Pepperoni kicked and fussed. Hardly any paint came off.

Aunt Sally took a look. "That's it," she said. "Go at it any longer, and you'll scrub the poor critter's hide right off its bones."

"But how can I show her at the fair, looking like that?" Tooter cried.

Aunt Sally shook her head sadly. "'Fraid you can't. Show's over for you two. Start planning for next year."

"No!" Tooter stomped into the house. She

called Jack Hafer on the phone. She told him what had happened. "You're the expert," she said. "How can I get this paint off my goat?"

Jack Hafer stopped laughing long enough to say, "You can't." Then he went on laughing.

Tooter hung up.

As the moon rose over the pasture, Tooter sat alone on the front porch. Gone was her dream of a blue ribbon. Gone also was her dream of seeing Jack Hafer's face when she showed up with her beautiful goat. She had imagined the crowd bursting into applause when she and Pepperoni appeared. She had imagined the judge crying out, "Hold it! Here's our winner!" And pinning the blue ribbon to her shirt...while Jack Hafer gawked in disbelief...

Dreams. Dashed.

Or were they?

Next morning Tooter couldn't find Chuckie in

his bed. Or at the breakfast table. She knew he was hiding from her.

She found him in the barn—and grabbed him.

"Mom!" he screamed. "She's gonna kill me!"

Tooter clamped his mouth shut. "Shh. I'm not going to kill you." She let him go. She smiled. "I just want to shake your hand."

"Huh?" said Chuckie.

Tooter shook his hand. "I just want to tell you what a great job you did painting my goat. She used to be so boring. Now she's…beautiful!"

Chuckie stared at her. "She *is*?"

"Yep," said Tooter. "In fact, you're so good at it, I think you should paint other people's goats too."

"You *do?*" said Chuckie.

"Yep," said Tooter. "Grab your paint and brush. Let's go!"

Tooter and Chuckie took a walk down Fox Hollow Road.

"Where are we going?" said Chuckie.

"Oh, I don't know," said Tooter. "We'll just walk till we come to a farm. Then we'll ask the farmer if he would like to have his goat painted."

"And it doesn't have to be stripes," said

Chuckie excitedly. "I can do polka dots too."

"Right," said Tooter. "Whatever you want."

Of course, Tooter knew exactly where they were going. And she had no intention of asking the farmer for permission to paint his goat.

Tooter had been awake half the night, thinking. She got madder each time she thought of Jack Hafer laughing. And winning another blue ribbon. Then it occurred to her: maybe he didn't have to win. Maybe something could happen to his goat too.

The Hafer farm was a mile down the road. "Hey, Chuckie, look!" Tooter cried when they came near. "There's a farm. I'll bet they have a boring goat that needs painting."

Chuckie raised his paintbrush. "Yeah!"

Tooter smiled. "I'll bet there's a goat behind that barn."

Chuckie started running. *"Ya-hoo!"*

Tooter watched her little brother race to Jack Hafer's farm. She saw him disappear behind the barn. But then—suddenly—he was back in view. He was racing toward her, screaming, terrified.

He grabbed her. "Tooter!" Hiding behind her, he pointed to the barn. "Dog! Bad dog!"

Tooter took his hand and pulled him along. When they reached the barn, Tooter heard a noise. It was a goat noise. *Maa-aa.* But different somehow. And louder.

Chuckie was whimpering, clutching her arm. Tooter crept along the side of the barn. The goat noise was getting louder. She reached back for a fistful of Chuckie's shirt.

She came to the end of the barn. She took a deep breath and peeked around the corner.

Coyote.

A scrawny, splotchy, brown, dog-looking

animal. Only three spits away from where she stood.

And Jack Hafer's goat, Cleo. Shaved creamy white for the show. Her head stuck in the fence again. Kicking and thrashing like a rodeo horse. The pom-pom a blur on the end of her tail. The coyote circling, circling, snapping at the flying hooves.

Tooter pulled back behind the corner. Her terrified eyes met Chuckie's terrified eyes. She couldn't move.

The goat was screaming.

She grabbed the paint can from Chuckie and charged into the barnyard. She screamed her lungs out—"YAAAAAAAAAAAA!" The coyote turned to look at her. She flung the

paint can. It clanked against the fence. By the time it settled in the barnyard dust, the intruder was gone.

Jack Hafer and his parents came running. "Cleo!" they yelled. "Cleo!" Jack went to his goat and worked its head loose from the fence.

Mrs. Hafer was looking down at Tooter, smiling. "You saved Cleo," she said. There were tears in her eyes.

Oh, no! What have I done? Tooter thought. *I saved Jack Hafer's goat!*

10

The Winner Is...

Tooter spent the next day at the county fair with her family. She passed the long tables of prize-winning vegetables and preserves. She didn't go anywhere near the goat show tent. She ended up spending all of her money on the bumper cars.

That night she stopped by her father's office. It was empty. She started up his computer. When she came to a blank screen, she began to type:

```
The girl and her goat,
Pepperoni Pepperday, worked
```

```
very hard. They really did.
But the girl's brother
painted Pepperoni with blue
stripes. And so the girl
could not enter the show.
It was very sad.
              The End
```

She turned off the computer and went to bed.

Next morning Tooter went to search for eggs. Feeling around in the darkness of the chicken coop, she heard a voice in the barnyard. Jack Hafer's. He was calling her name.

She knew why he was here. He had come to show off the blue ribbon he'd won. To wave it in her face. Who needed that? She crouched in the shadows of the coop.

But then Jack was in the doorway, peering in. "Tooter? You there?"

"No," she said.

"I can't see you. Come on out."

"I'm gathering eggs. Like the great farmer that I am."

He laughed. "Come on out anyway. I have something to show you."

"Don't bother. I know what it is."

"Tooter," he said. "Please."

Tooter gave in. She walked outside. Jack was standing there with a big grin on his face. And sure enough, he held a blue ribbon in his hand. He waved it in front of her.

"Big deal," she said. "If Pepperoni was there, you wouldn't have won."

Jack seemed to think about that. He shrugged. "Maybe not." He smiled. "Anyway, here—" He grabbed her hand and placed the blue ribbon in it. "This is yours as much as mine. For saving Cleo. I think you should have it."

Tooter stared at the ribbon. She didn't know what to say.

"Bye," said Jack, and ran to his bike.

When Jack disappeared down Fox Hollow Road, Tooter ran to the house. She came out with a hammer. She ran to the barn. She showed Pepperoni the blue ribbon. "This is yours too," she said. Pepperoni looked proud.

Tooter pulled a nail from her pocket. She tacked the blue ribbon onto the front post of the stall. She kissed Pepperoni on her proud, bony nose. "We'll take turns with it," she said. "You can have it the first week."

Then she raced into the house. "Dad! Dad!" she called as she flew up the stairs. Her father was at his usual place at the computer. He turned as she burst into the office. "Forget that ending I gave you," she gushed. "I have a new one." She jumped into his arms. "And *this* one is happy!"

Did you miss the first Tooter Tale?
Tooter learns about farm life the hard way in
Tooter Pepperday

"Goats have udders too?"

A terrible thought began to wriggle into Tooter's brain.

"But I drink milk every day."

Aunt Sally nodded. "I believe you do."

"And you're telling me the milk I drink comes from"—she pointed at the goat—"*that?*"

Aunt Sally answered cheerily: "That's why it's called goat's milk."

Tooter's tongue shot out as if trying to escape her mouth. She gagged. She stepped backward. She felt something mushy underfoot. She looked down at her sneaker. She looked up at Aunt Sally.

Aunt Sally nodded: "Goat poop."

ABOUT THE AUTHOR

None of Jerry Spinelli's six children was ever saddled with the responsibility of raising a chicken or training a goat, but his daughter Molly was just as persistent with him as Tooter Pepperday is with her father. While writing one of his books, Jerry didn't hear his daughter calling him until she sat on his desk and began writing him a note vertically along the page of his longhand manuscript! He told her to "Scoot!" but he did pay more attention to her the next time she came into the room.

Other books by Jerry Spinelli include *Fourth Grade Rats*, *The Bathwater Gang*, and *Maniac Magee*, for which he won the Newbery Medal in 1991. Jerry attended Gettysburg College. He lives with his wife, Eileen, also a children's book author, in Phoenixville, Pennsylvania.